MIDNIGHT IN
IN
MEMPHIS

Crabtree Publishing Company
www.crabtreebooks.com

PMB 16A, 350 Fifth Avenue
Suite 3308
New York, NY 10118

612 Welland Avenue
St. Catharines, Ontario
Canada, L2M 5V6

Bradman, Tony.
  Midnight in Memphis / Tony Bradman ; illustrated by Martin
Chatterton ; color by Ann Chatterton
      p. cm. -- (Blue Bananas)
  Summary: The Mummy family has to delay their vacation plans
when a flying saucer crashes into their pyramid and leaves a rock
star with amnesia to stay with them.
      ISBN 0-7787-0848-9 -- ISBN 0-7787-0894-2 (pbk.)
      [1. Mummies--Fiction. 2. Unidentified flying objects--Fiction. 3.
Humorous stories.] I. Chatterton, Martin, ill. II Title. III. Series.
PZ7.B7275 M1 2002
[E]--dc21

                           2001032439
                              LC

Published by Crabtree Publishing in 2002
First published in 1998 by Mammoth
an imprint of Egmont Children's Books Limited
Text copyright © Tony Bradman 1998
Illustrations copyright © Martin Chatterton 1998
The Author and Illustrator have asserted their moral rights.
Paperback ISBN 0-7787-0894-2
Reinforced Hardcover Binding ISBN 0-7787-0848-9

MIDNIGHT IN MEMPHIS

WRITTEN BY TONY BRADMAN
ILLUSTRATED BY MARTIN CHATTERTON
COLORED BY ANN CHATTERTON

Blue Bananas

To our Mummies
(and our Daddies)
M.C.

For
Ramona
T.B.

It was nighttime in The Land of Sand, and all the stars were twinkling. (Isn't that one twinkling a bit too brightly? Maybe not!)

It was quiet by the palm trees . . .

quiet at the

mummy police

station . . .

quiet in the ancient city of Memphis . . .

and quiet by

the pyramid.

(Isn't that star getting bigger and bigger?

Maybe not!)

And deep inside the pyramid it was very,
very quiet. That's where a family of
mummies was fast asleep!

But not for long . . .

In the morning the Mummies were going
on vacation. But now they were dreaming.

Then Daddy Mummy started to snore.

SNORE... SNORE... SNORE...

Soon there was another noise, too.

And suddenly there was a very loud . . .

The pyramid rocked, and everybody

woke up. The Mummies hugged each

other in fright.

What on Earth was that?

We'd better go and see!

I'm right behind you!

No, I'm right behind you!

Meow! Don't leave me here!

The Mummies went to the front door,

and stepped into the night.

A strange light shone down.

They looked up and saw . . .

a flying saucer! And it was sitting

on the top of the pyramid!

Lots of little green people came out of the flying saucer. The Mummies couldn't understand them. But they seemed very nice. There was a man with them too, and he was pretty confused.

Um... like have we landed yet?

Bibble!

Shmibble!

Bobble!

Dobble!

Guff!

Spooch!

The Mummies introduced themselves.

Then the Mummies discovered something

very odd. The man couldn't remember

his name, or where he lived.

Mommy Mummy and Daddy Mummy

felt sorry for him . . .

um... like, it's
a mystery
mummy
dudes.

. . . and said he could stay until his

memory returned. That pleased

the little green people.

They climbed into their flying saucer and left with a great big . . .

WHOOSH!

But when the sand settled . . .

. . . the Mummies were shocked. The pyramid looked different. In fact it had a GIGANTIC crack!

In the morning, the Mummies got up
and . . . didn't go on vacation. Mommy
Mummy and Daddy Mummy
tried to clean up. Their guest
just sat there whistling.

Mommy Mummy and Daddy Mummy

tried to fix the crack.

But it was just too difficult. So they

decided to call. . .

The Concrete Sisters. Their names were Cleo, Pat, and Nefertiti . . . and they were the best builders in The Land of Sand.

They came . . .

they tutted . . .

they measured . . .

they muttered . . .

and they shook their heads.

Then they wrote out an estimate.

The Concrete Sisters got
started right away.

DRRR! DRRR! DRRR!

They drilled
with their big drills.

BANG! BANG! BANG!

They hammered
with their
big
hammers.

DRRR! DRRR! DRRR!

They drilled with their big drills again.

But somebody seemed

to enjoy the noise.

Mommy Mummy and Daddy Mummy
were fed up.

They wished they were on vacation.

Their guest still couldn't remember

anything.

And The Concrete Sisters were making a

terrible mess.

But the Mummy kids were having fun.

They did lots of helping . . . and lots

of getting in the way.

Then Tut and Sis found some old bandages, and soon The Concrete Sisters were very wrapped up in their work!

That was enough for the Mummies. They

decided it was time to take their guest out.

So they all jumped in the mummy car.

Their guest hummed along to the

mummy radio . . .

. . . and they drove to the mummy police station.

Mommy Mummy asked if anyone had reported a missing man. But the mummy police couldn't help. They only dealt with missing mummies, not musical men with missing memories.

It was true, their guest was very musical . . .

The Mummies looked at each other.

They were in complete harmony.

And now they knew where to go. They

got everybody back into the mummy car

and headed for . . . Memphis.

They went straight to the mummy music

store. Tut and Sis ran in . . .

. . . and soon saw who their guest was!

The picture on the record cover struck a

chord with him, too.

um... like, that's me mummy dudes!

His name was Axle Grease, and he was a

star - a rock and roll one.

Axle remembered that he

had fallen over and bumped his head.

And that had made him

lose his memory.

The little green people had found him

 wandering around, and taken

him for a ride.

He's had a great time

with them. But he was glad to have his

memory back.

Axle was grateful to the Mummies for helping him. So later that evening, he gave a concert at the mummy music store.

It was midnight at Memphis, and everybody was there. Axle had a backup band that was way beyond compare.

The Concrete Sisters playing, the Mummies singing too, rocking and a-rolling with a mummy shoo-be-doo.

The concert was a great success. In fact, they made enough money to rebuild the pyramid . . .

That wasn't all, though. Axle said the Mummies deserved a vacation . . . and he arranged one for them. He took them to the mummy airport himself.

He seemed very,

very happy . . .

And suddenly Mommy

Mummy and Daddy

Mummy realized . . .

43

. . . they were on board the flying saucer with the little green people! The door started closing before they could get off.

And that's the end of the story

46